A catalogue record for this book is available
from the National Library of New Zealand

ISBN 978-1-988516-59-2

An Upstart Press Book
Published in 2019 by Upstart Press Ltd
Level 4, 15 Huron Street, Takapuna 0622
Auckland, New Zealand

Text and Illustrations © Stephanie Thatcher 2019
The moral rights of the author have been asserted.

Printed by Everbest Printing Co. Ltd., China

Everybody that met Polly
asked her if she wanted a cracker.

"Polly want a cracker?" they all asked.

PENGUINS

PANTHERS

PARROTS

PYTHONS

She most certainly did **not** want a cracker.
Crackers are dry and salty,
and altogether unpleasant.

Polly

They *could* have asked Polly if she would like
an ice-cream sundae, with sprinkles.

Or a lollipop.
She was rather fond of lollipops.

Or a delicious fruit salad,
with whipped cream and jelly!

But no, it was always a cracker.

"Polly want a cracker?"
they shouted.

And Polly always replied,

Polly

It is the only thing she has ever said,
because it is the only question she has ever been asked.

"Polly want a cracker?"

So the zookeeper declared that Polly was much too rude to live at the zoo, and sent her to live at a pet shop.

The pet shop was small and quiet,
with lots of dear little furry animals.

For Polly, however, it was the same old story. Every single person that came through the door asked Polly if she wanted a cracker.

"Polly want a cracker?"
they all asked.

The guinea pigs and kittens all hid in fear.

Then one day, Emma and her dad came into the pet shop.

Her father said, "Oh look, Emma, a parrot!
And she's called Polly! Polly want a cracker?"

shouted Polly in her shrillest voice.

He plodded off to look at the goldfish.

Emma looked up at Polly.

"I bet you don't even like crackers, do you Polly?" said Emma.
"I don't like crackers either, they're dry, and salty, and boring."

Polly was **very** surprised.
Nobody had ever spoken to her
like that before.

"Here, Polly," said Emma,

"would you like some of my lollipop?"

"Why, **yes!**" said Polly.
"Yes please, that would be delightful.
I would **love** some of your lollipop, please Emma."

It turned out that Polly
wasn't that rude after all.
She just didn't like crackers.

Polly

The pet-shop owner was only too happy
for Emma to take Polly home with her.

"It will be lovely to see the guinea pigs
and kittens again," she said.

Cat Treats

Now Polly and Emma are the best of friends.
They do everything together ...

and Emma never, EVER asks Polly
if she wants a cracker.